Contents

KU-635-653

People in the story

 **Sophia Reynolds** is going to be an extra in a film.

 **Fabio Facelli** is a famous film star.

 **George Cooper** is a policeman.

Places in the story

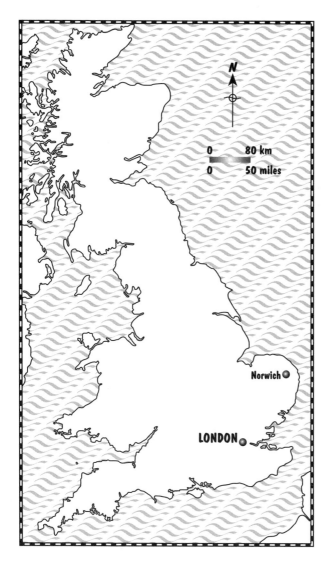

Chapter 1 *A bad start*

I'm here, in Norwich! Goodbye to my job in Jack's Café in London for six days! I feel very, very happy. I want to laugh and shout, and tell everyone about it.

I'm going to be in a film with Fabio Facelli! Yes, me, Sophia Reynolds, with Fabio Facelli! I *love* Fabio's films. And now I'm going to be in a film with him!

OK, it isn't just Fabio and me in the film. There are going to be lots of people. And I'm an 'extra'. I'm not going to speak, but I'm going to be in the film. With Fabio Facelli!

It's eight o'clock. I must be at Chapelfield Park at ten o'clock. I have two hours. First I can take my bag to my hotel.

I start to walk, but a woman stops me. 'Excuse me. Can you tell me how to get to Bank Street?' she asks.

I smile at the woman. 'I don't know Norwich, but I've got a map,' I tell her.

'Thank you,' says the woman.

The map is big and it's a windy day. My hair is over my face and I can't see. I try to find Bank Street. But the wind takes the map from my hands.

'Oh!' I start to laugh. The woman tries to help, but the wind is taking my map away.

'Come back here!' I shout and I run down the street after the map.

The map goes under a bus. I wait for the bus to stop. Then I go and get the map. I walk back up the street, but I can't see the woman. I look for her up and down the street. 'That's funny,' I think. I put the map back in my bag. Then I see that something's wrong.

'These aren't my things!' I say. 'This isn't my bag! Oh no, *she's* got my bag!'

I look up and down the street again, but the woman isn't there. I don't know what to do. Everything's going wrong. First the map, now my bag. Then I see something – a police station.

I take the woman's bag and start to run. I run to the police station, and I go in.

'My bag!' I shout at a policeman behind the desk. 'She's got my bag. You must help me. Please!'

Chapter 2 *Beautiful eyes*

The policeman doesn't look up at me. He's writing something. 'Sit down please, Miss,' he says.

I don't want to sit down. I want him to run into the street with me. I want him to help me. 'You don't understand!' I say. 'That bag's got all my things in it!'

The policeman looks up at me. I see he has beautiful, dark eyes. Not like Fabio's eyes, of course. But they are beautiful. What? Why am I thinking about this man's eyes? That woman's got my bag!

'All these people are waiting, Miss,' the policeman tells me. 'Please sit down.'

I look behind me. There are three or four people waiting. They all want to speak to the policeman too. 'But I must be at work by ten o'clock!' I try again, but the policeman just looks at me.

'Please, Miss,' he says.

'I know,' I say. 'Sit down.'

I go and sit down. And I wait. And wait. After thirty minutes, the policeman asks me to go over.

'Sit down, please,' he tells me. I sit.

'Name?' he asks.

'Sophia Reynolds.'

He writes it down. 'And how can we help you?'

I tell him about the woman and our bags. 'Now she's got my bag and I've got hers!' I say, and I give him the woman's bag.

He takes the bag from me and opens it. 'There's no name in here,' he says. 'We don't know how to find the woman.'

'What can we do?' I ask.

The policeman puts the bag down. 'You must leave it here,' he says.

'Now, tell me what's in your bag,' he says.

I tell him and he writes it all down.

'OK, Miss Reynolds,' he says. 'We must wait for the woman to come in. Come back this afternoon. Or phone us.' He writes the phone number down and gives it to me. 'Give me your number too,' he says. I give him my number and get up. 'Thank you,' I say. 'Goodbye.'

'Goodbye, Miss Reynolds,' he says, and then he looks away from me. 'Next please!' he calls.

A man comes over.

'Sit down, please,' the policeman says.

'Mr Sit Down,' I think. 'That's a good name for you!'

Chapter 3   *Mr Sit Down*

Out in the street I look for Chapelfield Park on my map. Good – it's not far. I can get there by ten o'clock. I start to walk. Then I hear something and look down. A small boy is next to me. He looks about three or four. And he's crying.

'Hello,' I say. 'Where's your mother?'

The boy doesn't answer. He just cries.
I take his hand. 'Don't cry,' I say.

I look up and down the street, but I can't see the boy's mother. I know what to do. I smile at the boy.

'Come on,' I say. 'Come and see Mr Sit Down with me. He's a policeman.'

The boy walks with me down the street. He doesn't stop crying. We go into the police station and everyone looks at us. The boy is crying loudly.

My policeman is speaking to a woman at his desk. I take the boy over to the desk and the policeman looks up.

'Miss Reynolds,' the policeman says.

I speak fast. 'This boy can't find his mother,' I tell him.

'Excuse me,' the policeman says to the woman at his desk. He gets up and comes over to the boy. His face is kind. 'What's your name?' he asks the boy.

The boy stops crying. 'Peter,' he says. Then he looks at the policeman. 'Are you Mr Sit Down?' he asks.

'Oh help!' I think.

The policeman looks at me. His eyes are smiling. I want to die.

'I'm PC George Cooper,' he tells the boy.

'George,' I think. 'His name's George.'

Then a woman runs into the police station.

'Peter!' she shouts. 'Peter!' She runs over to the boy.
Peter starts crying again. 'Mummy!' he says.

George gets up. He smiles at me. I smile too. Everyone is happy.

'Thank you for your help, Miss Reynolds,' George says.

'Excuse me,' says the woman at George's desk. 'I must be at work in ten minutes.'

Work! The film! I'm going to be late!

'Goodbye,' I say to George. 'See you this afternoon.' And I run out of the police station.

Chapter 4   *Two angry men*

I wait to go across the street. There are lots of cars. I start to think about Fabio Facelli. Is he in Chapelfield Park now?

There's a red car coming very fast. The car in front of it stops, and the fast red car drives into it. Crash!

I run over to the front car. The window is open. 'Are you OK?' I ask the man in the car.

'My new car!' the man says. He gets out. He looks at his car. Then he goes over to the red car behind. He starts to shout at the man in the red car. 'Look at my car!'

The man in the red car gets out. He looks angry too. 'Look at *my* car!' he says.

I look at them. Oh no! I don't want to go into the police station again! I *can't* go in there again! But the men are shouting now. People are stopping and looking. Why don't they go into the police station for help? But they don't.

So I go.

George is at his desk. 'Miss Reynolds!' he says.

'Please come,' I say. 'There's going to be a fight!'

George gets up quickly and comes with me.

There's a lot of noise out in the street. The two men are fighting now. I don't like it. They're big men and they're very angry. George runs over. I watch George at work. I don't know why, but I think about Fabio Facelli in his film *Bad Men Die*.

Fabio Facelli! The film! I must get to Chapelfield Park now!

I leave George with the angry men and run up the street.

Chapter 5 *Shouting for Fabio*

I get to Chapelfield Park at 9.59. I'm not late, but I don't look good. Because of the wind, my hair is everywhere. It *is* a bad hair day. But by 10.30 I don't look like Sophia Reynolds. *Beautiful Young Things* is a 1960s film, and all the extras have 1960s hair.

'From bad hair day to big hair day!' I think.

In the film Fabio Facelli is a famous singer, Ricky Burns. All the extras are going to watch him sing. I can't believe it – in a minute I'm going to see Fabio Facelli!

'OK,' says the film director. 'You're all here to see the famous Ricky Burns. You *love* Ricky Burns! And any minute he's going to be here! I want you all to shout for Ricky. OK!'

Everyone starts to shout. 'Ricky! Ricky!'

Then a man comes over. He's tall with dark hair and beautiful eyes. 'Fabio!' I start to shout. Fabio!'

'Stop!' says the film director.

'Shout out for Ricky, not Fabio, please!' the director says.

'Oh no!' I think.

'Sorry, Fabio,' the film director says to the tall man with dark hair.

Fabio Facelli's eyes look cold. 'That's funny,' I think, 'they never look cold in his films.' He walks away again.

'OK!' says the film director and we start to shout again.

This time I shout out, 'Ricky!'

We shout and shout and shout. After thirty minutes I can't talk because of all the shouting.

'OK,' says the film director to us. 'We're going to stop for ten minutes and have a drink.'

I have a drink and then I go to find my phone. I want to phone George about my bag. But I've got a text from him. He's got my bag!

'OK, everyone!' I hear the director shout.

I put my phone away and run out. Crash! I run into a man. It's Fabio Facelli!

'Why don't you look where you're going?' Fabio shouts at me. 'Look at my trousers!'

'Sorry,' I start to say. But Fabio doesn't stop to listen.

I watch him go. 'You have beautiful eyes,' I think, 'but you're not a beautiful man.' Then I think about another man's eyes. Dark eyes. PC George Cooper's eyes.

Chapter 6   *A George Cooper film*

We stop work at five o'clock. What a day! I feel very tired.

I walk slowly to the police station to get my bag. Next to the police station, a man speaks to me.

'Miss Reynolds? Is that you?'

I look up and see a man on a big motorbike. It's George!

I smile and go up to him. 'Thank you for your text,' I say.

He smiles at me. He looks very good in black on his motorbike. 'I'm just doing my job, Miss Reynolds.'

He's looking at my hair. Is that why he's smiling like that? Or does he like me?

'Please call me Sophia,' I tell him.

'Well, thank you for your help today, Sophia,' he says. He looks at my hair again. 'Your hair is very ... big this evening,' he says.

I laugh. 'Yes,' I say. 'I'm having a big hair day! They're making a film in Chapelfield Park. I'm an extra in it.'

'You're going to be famous then?' he asks.

I think about Fabio Facelli and his cold eyes. But George is smiling at me and I don't feel sad. 'No,' I say, 'I'm not going to be famous.'

George looks at me. 'Are you going to get your bag?' he asks.

'Yes,' I say, but I don't want to walk away from him. I don't want him to go.

Does he know what I'm thinking? 'Do you want to go for a drink?' he asks. 'Get your bag first. I can wait for you.'

I smile a very big smile. 'Yes,' I say. 'Yes, please!'

'Good,' he says.

We don't just have a drink. We talk and we laugh a lot. And he kisses me. It feels like a film, when the boy gets the girl. Only this isn't a Fabio Facelli film, it's a George Cooper film.

George Cooper films are *very* good!